BE
BLEST

*Heartfelt thanks to Pat, my parents, and Liz and John Hughes for
my trip to Assisi. Special thanks to Mary Chase for help with the musical
arrangement for "Be Blest," and to Paul for his loving support.*

SIMON & SCHUSTER BOOKS FOR YOUNG READERS
An imprint of Simon & Schuster Children's Publishing Division
1230 Avenue of the Americas, New York, New York 10020

Calligraphy by Jan Owen
Book design by Mary Beth Owens and Lily Malcom
The text of this book is set in Tiepolo.
The paintings were executed in Winsor Newton watercolors
on Strathmore 500-plate surface illustration board.
Printed in Hong Kong
10 9 8 7 6 5 4 3 2 1

Library of Congress Cataloging-in-Publication Data
Owens, Mary Beth.
Be blest : a celebration of seasons / Mary Beth Owens.—1st ed.
p.   cm.
Summary: Presents prayers for each of the months of the year, including
search-and-find paintings of plants, animals, and insects.
ISBN 0-689-80546-2 (hc)
1. Children—Prayer-books and devotions—English. 2. Seasons—Religious aspects—
Juvenile literature. [1. Prayers. 2. Seasons—Religious aspects. 3. Nature— Religious
aspects. 4. Picture puzzles.] I. Title.
BL625.5.O84 1999
291.4'33—dc21
98-49038

For Pat—

"I said to the almond tree,
'sister, speak to me of God,'
and the almond tree
blossomed."

—N. Kazantzakis

Be Blest

A Celebration of Seasons

Mary Beth Owens

Simon & Schuster Books for Young Readers

Author's Note

This book was inspired by Saint Francis of Assisi's "Canticle of Brother Sun." Francis recognized God's presence in all things and saw relationships between people, animals of the fields and forests, birds, fish, insects, trees, flowers, stones, the sun, moon and stars, fire and water, rain and snow, light and dark. All were included in his family circle, as brothers and sisters.

While working on *Be Blest*, I came across the work of Gaelic scholar Alexander Carmichel, who collected prayers and blessings from the Celtic oral tradition at the end of the nineteenth century. In these prayers the spiritual and natural worlds are intertwined. God's presence is acknowledged and honored in the rhythm, textures, and colors of the seasons; in the daily pattern of work, play, sleeping, and waking.

When we align ourselves with the natural world, God is present for us. Through prayer we can expand our awareness of the "other." Blessings are given and received when we pay attention to the relationships among all forms of life. Praise and thanksgiving are the natural responses of a mind that knows the created world and a heart that is filled with gratitude. Rejoicing follows from the recognition of all the gifts around us.

With this book I celebrate the creative power that pervades the natural world and my connection to it.

Be Blest, Sing Praise,
Rejoice, Give Thanks,
the seasons circle 'round,
and God's good gifts
for all are near
in plenty to be found.

Be Blest
when wind and ice
shake seeds
from lifeless plants
and tattered weeds.
On barren branches
leaf buds bear
the promise of
another year.

January

Be Blest
in winter's rest
when groundhog slumbers,
squirrels nest;
for sister bear
with bulbs asleep,
while spring lies hidden
in her keep.

February

Sing Praise,
when pussy willows show
and daffodils push
through the snow.
The sunlight
the mourning cloaks
have sought
warms sister hare,
twixt seasons caught.

March

Sing Praise

with peepers
all night long
beside the sprouting
cattail pond,
while mallard nests
with watchful eye,
and wood frogs sing
their lullaby.

April

Sing Praise

around the apple tree
when blossoms stir
with honeybees.
Above in branches
robins nest;
below, the earth wakes
from her rest.

May

Rejoice!
Up from the earth
they rise,
cabbagemoths and butterflies.
Cicadas, lacewings,
crickets sing,
while swallows dance
on quickened wings.

June

Rejoice
under the summer moon,
with honeysuckle vines
in bloom,
for creatures moving
in the night,
surrounded by the
fireflies' light.

July

Rejoice
in fields
beneath the sky
on radiant wings
of damselfly,
who sees
ripe berries
everywhere,
enough to eat,
enough to share.

August

Give Thanks
in orchards
at harvesttime,
for fruiting tree
and ripened vine,
where brother groundhog
tries to keep
his belly full
for winter's sleep.

September

Give Thanks
for autumn's golden glow,
in step of deer
and cry of crow.
When cold winds whisper
frost and snow,
the wild geese know
it's time to go.

October

Give Thanks

within the sheltered place,
for seeds and roots
and mossy space.
Contained in every
season's end:
the blessing to begin again.

November

Be Blest
when snow reveals
her tales
in weasel, deer
and foxes' trails—
whom owl has met,
where deer mice go . . .
concealing all
when snowdrifts blow.

December

Be Blest

(Refrain) Joyfully

Mary Beth Owens

Be blest, sing praise, re - joice, give thanks, the sea - sons cir - cle 'round, And God's good gifts for

all are near in plen - ty to __ be found, In plen - ty to be found.

(*Verse)

Be blest for sun __ and moon and stars, sing praise for wind __ and air, Re -

To Refrain

joice with wa - ter, fire, and earth, Give thanks for crea - tures, ev - 'ry-where.

* Verses on previous pages should be substituted for appropriate season.